DR JACQUELINE MITTON holds an M.A. in Physics from the University of Oxford and a Doctorate in Astrophysics from the University of Cambridge. A distinguished writer on astronomy, she is also the Press Officer for the Royal Astronomical Society, a position she has held since 1989. She is a Fellow of the Royal Astronomical Society and a Member of the International Astronomical Union. In 1990, Asteroid 4027 was named 'Mitton' after Jacqueline and her husband, Simon. A prolific author on astronomy, she has written or co-authored 9 books for children and 10 for adults, and has contributed to several children's encyclopedias. Her recent books include *The Cambridge Dictionary of Astronomy* and *The Young Oxford Encyclopedia of Science: Stars and Planets*. *The Marshall Children's Guide to Astronomy* (with Simon Mitton) was shortlisted for the Rhône Poulenc Junior Science Book Prize 1999. She has collaborated with Christina Balit on three previous titles: *Zoo in the Sky* and *Kingdom of the Sun*, both of which have won awards, and *Zodiac: Celestial Circle of the Sun*.

CHRISTINA BALIT studied at Chelsea School of Art and the Royal College of Art. She is also a playwright, and her involvement with fringe theatre has strongly influenced her illustrative work. She did the illustrations for the Lion Bible. Her first book for Frances Lincoln, Michael Morpurgo's *Blodin the Beast*, was shortlisted for the 1995 Kate Greenaway Medal and in 1996 *Ishtar and Tammuz*, written by Christopher Moore, was Commended for the Kate Greenaway Medal. Among Christina's other books are James Riordan's *The Twelve Labours of Hercules*, Mary Hoffman's *Women of Camelot* and Robert Leeson's *My Sister Shahrazad*. Christina is both author and illustrator of *Atlantis: The Legend of a Lost City* and *Escape from Pompeii*. Her collaboration with Jacqueline Mitton on *Zoo in the Sky: A Book* won the U.S. Parents' Guide to Children's Media Award, and their next collaboration *Kingdom of the Sun: A Book of the Planets,* was the winner of the 2002 English Association 4-11 Book Award for Key Stage 2 Non-Fiction. It was followed by *Once Upon a Starry Night* and *Zodiac*.

NORTHERN SKY

This star map has the North Celestial Pole as its centre. It shows constellations of the northern sky. Constellations lying across the celestial equator appear on both maps. Paler areas represent the Milky Way.

Constellations on the map of the northern sky featured in this book:

Andromeda

Cassiopeia

Cepheus

Hercules

Lyra – the Lyre

Ophiuchus

Orion

Pegasus

Perseus

+ marks the Celestial Pole

SOUTHERN SKY

This star map has the South Celestial Pole as its centre. It shows constellations of the southern sky. Constellations lying across the celestial equator appear on both maps. Paler areas represent the Milky Way.

Constellations on the map of the southern sky featured in this book:

Carina – the Keel

Centaurus

Ophiuchus

Orion

Puppis – the Stern

Vela – the Sail

Note: Astronomers have divided the very large old constellation Argo into Carina (the Keel), Puppis (the Stern) and Vela (the Sail)

*TriA=Triangulum Australe
+ marks the Celestial Pole

FOR SIMON – J.M.
FOR MY SISTERS AMIRA AND DANNI – C.B.

First published in Great Britain in 2003 by
Frances Lincoln Limited, 4 Torriano Mews
Torriano Avenue, London NW5 2RZ
www.franceslincoln.com

First paperback edition published in 2005

British Library Cataloguing in Publication Data
available on request

ISBN 1-84507-073-9

Printed in China
9 8 7 6 5 4 3 2 1

ONCE UPON A STARRY NIGHT

Heroes and Gods of the Constellations

Jacqueline Mitton

Christina Balit

FRANCES LINCOLN

THE LAST HINTS of pink and orange have faded in the west. Darkness creeps across the clear sky like a velvet curtain. It's a perfect night for telling a story.

But what about some pictures to go with the story? Look up, and what do you see? Not just stars, but a vast picture-book. The night sky is a realm of kings and queens, gods, heroes and mystical creatures. Look – they're all there, outlined by the stars. You only need a little imagination . . .

CASSIOPEIA

Where the Milky Way tumbles through the northern sky sits Queen Cassiopeia, a zigzag of dazzling stars, with Cepheus her king close by.

"See how beautiful I am," she declared one day, "fairer than all the nymphs of the sea."

Poseidon was angry with Cassiopeia. "No mortal insults my nymphs!" said the ocean god. "I'll punish you for your vanity." And he sent a frightful sea monster to terrify the kingdom.

ANDROMEDA

Andromeda is King Cepheus' beloved daughter. A spiral galaxy lies just beside her and the blue and yellow gem of a double star flashes on her skirt.

"Sacrifice your daughter – it's the only way to stop the beast," her father was told. So the princess was chained to rocks by the sea to await her horrible fate.

Her heart beat fast with fear. Would anyone help her before it was too late?

PERSEUS

Perseus to the rescue! Winged sandals on his feet, the hero speeds through the Milky Way to Andromeda's side. He carries the fearsome head of Medusa, the ghastly Gorgon he has slain. The Demon Star that is Medusa's eye winks eerily. Perseus holds high his magic sickle, twin star clusters glistening beside his hand.

"Death to the sea monster!" he cries.

So Andromeda was saved and bold Perseus married his princess.

PEGASUS

Pegasus the heavenly horse soars gracefully overhead, four bright stars at the corners of his Great Square.

After Perseus had killed Medusa, Pegasus sprang up where her blood had fallen. Faithfully the winged horse served the mighty god Zeus, carrying his thunder and lightning.

When the mortal Bellopheron mounted Pegasus and tried to ride him to the realm of the gods, angry Zeus flung him back to earth – but rewarded Pegasus for his loyal service by setting him in the stars.

LYRA

High in the sky, a great bird bears the lyre of Orpheus, adorned with bright stars and a wispy ring of gleaming gas.

Orpheus' singing left his listeners spellbound and the music of his lyre held them like a charm.

Grief-stricken after his young wife died, he softened the hearts of the underworld gods with his music.

"Your wife may follow you to the land of the living," they decreed, "so long as you do not look at her on the way." But Orpheus couldn't resist glancing back – and she was gone for ever.

HERCULES

Immortalised by the gods, Hercules the superhero kneels in the sky, a clustering ball of stars at his thigh.

Renowned for his many feats of strength, Hercules (called Herakles by the Ancient Greeks) could not be harmed by sword or fire because of the miraculous lion-skin he wore. He didn't fear the fiery dragon who guarded the golden apples of the Hesperides. For one of his famous labours he seized the apples – and crushed the dragon with his foot!

ORION

Striding boldly through the heavens comes the brilliant hunter Orion.

Son of the sea-god Poseidon, he could walk on water and was tall enough to wade through the ocean. So great a huntsman was this handsome giant, even the goddess Artemis deigned to hunt with him. But when he dared to touch her, Artemis was furious and her punishment speedy: Orion died from a scorpion's sting.

Now starry pearls stud his belt and where his sword hangs, a haze of glowing gas glistens.

CENTAURUS

Chiron the Centaur – half-man, half-horse – trots along the Milky Way.

Clever and kind, wise and fair, immortal Chiron was a wonderful teacher and healer. Then by chance a poisoned arrow struck him, and there was no cure.

"This pain is too great to bear for ever," he cried. He begged to die, and Zeus granted his wish, giving him an honoured place in the sky.

Now a fuzzy swarm of a million stars rides on the Centaur's back. Our nearest bright star, Alpha Centauri, burns yellow at his foot.

ARGO

"Bring me the sacred golden fleece!" commanded Jason's scheming uncle (secretly thinking, "He'll die if he tries"). But undeterred, Jason and fifty friends set off in the great ship *Argo* on their dangerous adventure.

"To win the Fleece, first yoke my fiery bulls and sow these dragon's teeth," demanded the king who owned the Fleece. "Then fight the soldiers who spring up where the teeth fall." Impossible? No! With magical help, Jason won the Fleece.

Now the *Argo* sails a sea of stars as three constellations: keel, stern and sail.

Stars, nebulas and galaxies

The stars are like our Sun: huge balls of glowing gas. They look like small specks of light only because they are very far away. Some of the specks we see shining in the night sky look fuzzy. They are often called 'nebulas' – from the Latin word for clouds. But there are several different kinds of fuzzy objects. Some really are bright clouds of gas; others are families of stars. You can tell the difference when you look at them through a telescope.

We are in a galaxy of thousands of millions of stars: all the stars we see at night belong to it. The Milky Way is the light of many distant stars. Our galaxy is shaped like a disc with a bulge in the middle and spiral arms winding out from the bulge. It is a great island of stars in space and just one of billions of galaxies in the universe.

Constellations

The stars in a constellation look near to each other in the sky, but they are not really close together: they are scattered in space, all at different distances from us. When we say that a star is "in a constellation", it tells us where to find it on the sky, not where it is in space.

The whole sky is divided up between 88 different-sized constellations, just as a continent is divided into countries or states. Every star, star cluster, nebula or galaxy belongs to one of the constellations.

The official names of constellations are in Latin, though some of their names come from characters in Greek myths. This book uses the Greek names for the gods and goddesses who appear in the stories.

More about some night sky objects in this book

ANDROMEDA

The spiral galaxy in Andromeda is the most distant thing you can see without a telescope and the nearest large galaxy to our own. It is more than 2 million light years away, which means that the light we pick up from it now set out from the galaxy over 2 million years ago. Our Milky Way Galaxy is similar to the Andromeda galaxy, but not quite as large.

PERSEUS

The second brightest star in Perseus is called Algol or the Demon Star. Regular as clockwork, every 2 days 20 hours and 49 minutes it dims noticeably, then brightens again. In reality, Algol is a pair of stars going around each other. Normally we see their combined light, but when the fainter star crosses in front of the brighter one, it cuts out some of the light, and the pair looks fainter.

In Perseus you can also see the famous double star cluster, visible without a telescope. The two clusters are almost twins, and only about 50 light years apart, although over 7,000 light years away.

LYRA

Stars don't stay the same for ever. They can last billions of years, but when they grow old, they change. In Lyra, there's an old star that swelled up into a giant, then puffed off its outside, like a shell, about 7,000 years ago. It formed a nebula called the Ring Nebula around what is left of the old star. You need a telescope to see it.

HERCULES

Some of the oldest stars in our Galaxy can be found in tight, ball-shaped swarms of stars that astronomers call globular clusters. In Hercules you will find the brightest globular cluster in the northern half of the sky. Known simply as M13, it has no other name. About 300,000 stars are packed in this cluster, which is over 20,000 light years away. You can see it without a telescope.

ORION

Glowing gas around a group of bright young stars forms the famous Orion Nebula in the Hunter's sword. Behind the Nebula lurks a huge dark cloud of gas and dust 1,300 light years away. This is a birthplace of stars. No more than a hundred thousand years ago, the stars in the Orion Nebula began to shine, blasting through the dark cloud with their rays and lighting up the gas around them. The Nebula is visible without a telescope.

CENTAURUS

Centaurus is home to the brightest and biggest of all globular star clusters. Called Omega Centauri, it is 16,500 light years away and 620 light years across. You can easily see it without a telescope.

The brightest star in this constellation, Alpha Centauri, is the nearest bright star to the Sun. In reality it is a double star, just over 4 light years away. The two stars slowly waltz around each other once every 80 years. A very dim star in Centaurus, called Proxima, is a tiny bit nearer to us than Alpha.

ARGO

The huge southern constellation Argo Navis (the Ship *Argo*) existed for about 2,000 years. Then, in 1930, it was officially split into three when astronomers agreed to divide up the sky into 88 constellations. The parts of Argo are Carina (the Keel), Puppis (the Stern) and Vela (the Sail). But long before 1930, astronomers had been using these names for the different parts of Argo. The star Canopus, the brightest in Carina, is the second brightest in the whole sky. Also in Carina lies a lovely, brilliant cluster of 30 newly-formed stars, quite different from the old globular clusters. Although the cluster doesn't have a special name, it's easy to see without a telescope.

NORTHERN SKY

This star map has the North Celestial Pole as its centre. It shows constellations of the northern sky. Constellations lying across the celestial equator appear on both maps. Paler areas represent the Milky Way.

Constellations on the map of the northern sky featured in this book:

Andromeda

Cassiopeia

Cepheus

Hercules

Lyra – the Lyre

Ophiuchus

Orion

Pegasus

Perseus

+ marks the Celestial Pole

Pegasus

Cetus

Aquarius

Mira

Taurus

Fomalhaut

Altair

Phoenix

Grus

Capricornus

Eridanus

Achernar

Tucana

Aquila

Rigel

Dorado

Hydrus

Pavo

Sagittarius

Serpens Cauda

Columba

Volans +Apus

Ara

Lepus

Canopus

Musca

TriA*

Betelgeuse

Carina

Rigil Kent

Antares

Sirius

Crux

Ophiuchus

Canis Major

Vela

Lupus

Scorpius

Puppis

Centaurus

Procyon

Libra

Canis Minor

Serpens Caput

Hydra

Corvus

Spica

Regulus

Virgo

This star map has the South Celestial Pole as its centre. It shows constellations o the southern sky. Constellations lying across the celestial equator appea on both maps. Paler area represent the Milky Way

Constellations on the map o the southern sky feature in this book

Carina – the Kee

Centaurus

Ophiuchus

Orion

Puppis – the Stern

Vela – the Sai

Note: Astronomers have divided the very large old constellation Argo into Carina (the Keel), Puppis (the Stern and Vela (the Sail)

*TriA=Triangulum Australe
+ marks the Celestial Pole

MORE PICTURE BOOKS FROM FRANCES LINCOLN

ZOO IN THE SKY
A Book of Animal Constellations
Jacqueline Mitton

Illustrated by Christina Balit

Drawing on the lure of the heavens, this introduction to the night sky, stars and galaxies
includes maps of the Southern and Northern skies charting the history of the constellations and the Milky Way.
Winner of the U.S. Parents' Guide to Children's Media Award.

ISBN 0-7112-1319-4

KINGDOM OF THE SUN
A Book of the Planets
Jacqueline Mitton

Illustrated by Christina Balit

Which planet has a spiralling storm that has raged for hundreds of years? Which planet dashes around the Sun
faster than any other? A lyrical text accompanied by magical paintings takes a fascinating tour of the planets
of our Solar System. Winner of the 2002 English Association 4-11 Book Award for Key Stage 2 Non-Fiction.

ISBN 0-7112-1947-8

ZODIAC
Celestial Circle of the Sun
Jacqueline Mitton

Everyone knows their own star sign, but how many people can identify the Zodiac constellations in the night sky
and the stars that form them? Here is an astronomical guide to the Zodiac and to the celestial legends of gods,
mortal men and fantasy creatures in which the age-old tradition is rooted.

ISBN 1-84507-074-7

Frances Lincoln titles are available from all good bookshops.
You can also buy books and find out more about your favourite titles,
authors and illustrators at our website: www.franceslincoln.com.